Snow Angels

A Christmas Story

Written by **ANDREW GLASS**

Illustrated by **KATHY NAUSLEY**

SANDY CREEK

For Katherine Elvira—A. G.

In memory of my father, who reached for his dreams so
that I might achieve mine—K. N.

Text © 2008 by Andrew Glass.
Illustrations © 2008 by Kathy Nausley.

This 2008 edition published by Sandy Creek,
by arrangement with St. Martin's Press.

Designed by Barbara Grzeslo

Sandy Creek
122 Fifth Avenue
New York, NY 10011

ISBN-13: 978-1-4351-0158-6

Printed and bound in Thailand

1   3   5   7   9   10   8   6   4   2

*Seeing an angel, wings and all,
is as rare as finding a pearl in your oyster stew.*

All morning, the twins, fresh from down south, stared out the windows of McCurdle Elementary. The softly falling flakes were the first snow Emily and Harold had ever seen—and a Christmas Eve snowstorm, to boot!

Bing-bong!—An announcement boomed from the loudspeaker: "Due to hazardous snow conditions, afternoon classes will be cancelled. Happy holidays!"

Emily and Harold bumped and jostled to be first
through the tall door. The playground was like a cloud.
The trees looked like sparkling dinosaurs. Parked cars were
buffalo mounds along the lacy schoolyard fence.

The twins dropped their backpacks and flopped into the heavenly snow. They stretched their arms and legs back and forth, back and forth. Everyone joined in, and soon the schoolyard was aflutter.

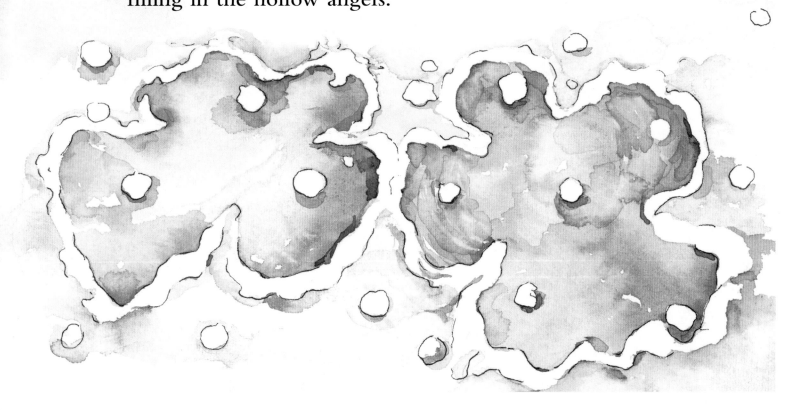

Then the kids all scrambled home.

Emily looked over her shoulder. Snow was already filling in the hollow angels.

Noah sat up first, stuck out his tongue, and caught
a snowflake. It tingled. One by one, all the angels in the
schoolyard sat up, too. They giggled with delight as frosty
air stung their noses and colored their cheeks.

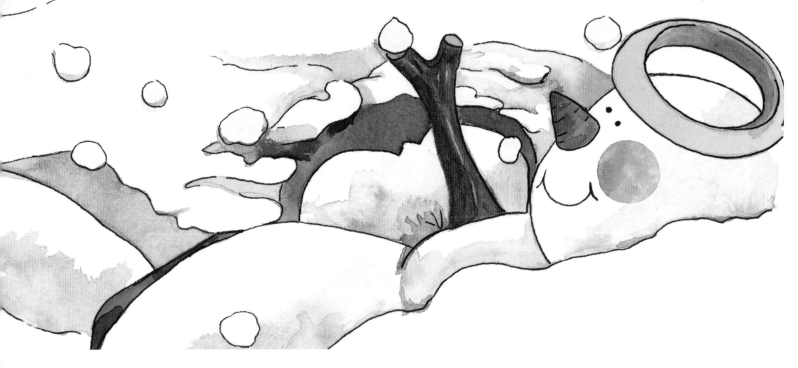

Soon, children ran outside, bundled to the ears and
dragging sleds. The angels raced along, crunching paths
through the snow, dazzled by colored boots and bright
scarves, sparkling eyes and slippery shouts.

Emily and Harold kept up, sliding their brand-new sled smoothly over the drifts. Just ahead, Fishers Hill swirled like a bakery cake all the way down to Fishers Creek, flowing chilly beneath an icy crust of snow.

Everyone shared sleds and disks and stubby skis,
gliding giddy as penguins down the hill.

Angels and children don't have a chipmunk's notion of time when they're having fun. So they didn't notice the hillside, white and soft and safe as a blanket, becoming a swirling, drifting, growling polar bear. No one heard the anxious calls either: "Time to come home!"

Harold and Emily raced madly past the others, sailing down splendid snowdrifts all the way to Fishers Creek, as the howling blizzard overtook them all.

Shivering children searched the twirling darkness for rooftops or fence posts or some familiar landmark to guide them back to their warm houses. But churning snow buried every clue.

What happened next is hard to say. The children claimed they followed a path of twinkling Christmas lights, floating high as a clothesline all the way back up the hill through the storm to McCurdle Elementary, and right to their doors. Before long, they were safely sipping steaming hot chocolate in cozy kitchens telling an unbelievable story.

Angels tumbled and twirled like whirlwinds before
flopping down in the schoolyard, stretching their arms and
legs back and forth, back and forth. "Merry Christmas,"
they whispered, "Merry Christmas." One by one, they
disappeared, until only Noah, who felt like he'd forgotten
something, was left.

"Emily, time to come home!" Noah sat very still, listening. "Emily, Harold, where are you?" That's what he'd forgotten: those twins with the new sled! They'd sailed right past him, headed straight for Fishers Creek. He jumped to his feet and flew, beating his wings as fast as he could.

He found them clinging to each other on a crust of ice so thin they could feel the chilly creek flowing under their boots and biting their toes. The wind had spun them until they didn't know which way to go. So they stood very still. But when the howling bully of a blizzard snatched Harold's new hat, both children stretched and stumbled, trying to snatch it back. That was the moment Noah took Emily's hand and reached for Harold's, too, just as the ice cracked.

Emily's boots dipped into the chilly creek. She thought she felt Harold tug hard to pull her from the icy water. "Don't let go!" she shouted.

"Don't worry, I won't!" said Harold. He couldn't see a thing through the swirling snow. So he believed his sister was guiding him across the ice with a sure grip.

Emily could barely feel her frozen feet. Slipping and sliding up the hill, clutching Harold's hand, felt like flying. She even heard the flutter of strong wings. She turned and squinted through her eyelashes. But it could only have been the blizzard beating against her cheeks. She hung on, spinning with the storm, until she saw Dad at the end of the driveway calling, "Harold, Emily!"

The twins tumbled in snowy heaps right at the door
on their own back porch.

"We're home," called Emily, stomping her feet.

"Snow is unbelievable," Harold shouted, letting the door slam. Mom hung up the phone and hugged them. "Thank goodness!"

A few minutes later, the porch light blinked off.

Between sips of hot chocolate, Emily said, "Harold held my hand firmly like a hero. We practically flew home."

"Emily's the hero," said Harold. "She knew the way and didn't let go."

Mom and Dad were much too happy that the twins were home safely to wonder why their stories didn't match. And Emily never said a word.

But later, she opened the back door just a crack, barely enough for a tall mug to slip through from the bright kitchen into the cold darkness.

Emily peered after it. She didn't dare turn on the light. So she may have just imagined the angel on the back porch.

Hot chocolate tasted sweet and warm,
like Christmas.